Wonderful Short Stories about Boys

Inspiring Confidence, Kindness, Honesty, and to Go on Dreaming

Alice Elton

TABLE OF CONTENTS

YOUR FREE GIFTS

As a way of saying thanks for your purchase, I'm offering these books Inspiring Short Stories of Fascinating Animals and Basel Kid Detective Riddle and Puzzle Books for FREE to my readers.

To get instant access just go to:

https://springloftpublishing.com/free-gifts

Inside these books, you'll get:

- More entertaining short stories with powerful life lessons.
- Riddles and Puzzle book you can exercise your brain too.
- And more fun for the whole family!

If you want more inspiring stories and a good mind-twister, make sure to grab these freebies.

A MESSAGE TO THE ASPIRING YOUNG READER

Do you enjoy reading stories?

If you have a big imagination and enjoy bedtime stories, prepare to be delighted with this collection of short stories for little boys.

While growing up, you need to learn many things like being confident, responsible, and honest. But when grown-ups try to explain these values, it might be a bit difficult to understand them. Through these stories, you will discover the true meaning of different values and why they're so important.

These tales are about little boys like you who go on adventures, learn valuable lessons, and even make some new friends along the way. Read one story each day or read them all from start to finish!

With each tale, you will meet new characters, little boys who are just like you.

If you're ready to start reading, turn the page, and have fun!

Dream Big,
Little One

If you can dream it, you can do it.
—WALT DISNEY

Benny was a little boy who lived in a small town. He was friendly and cheerful, and he liked to daydream a lot. But all the other boys and girls in his town didn't have time to daydream. They just wanted to play and have fun.

One morning, when Benny arrived at school, he saw someone new.

The little girl was a bit tall, had fair skin, and had bright red curly hair. The little boy wondered who she was. He wondered if she was a new student in the school. He wondered if she would be in his class.

"Good morning, Ms. Molly," Benny said as he went inside his classroom.

Before Ms. Molly could say anything, the bell rang. So she smiled at him and gave him a nod. The little boy smiled back at her before going to his seat.

"Today is going to be an exciting day. You will soon meet someone new. She is an exchange student from a different country and she will be with us for one month," Ms. Molly said.

Benny thought about the girl he saw outside. He wondered if she was the one Ms. Molly was talking about. Just then, someone knocked on the door. When the teacher opened the door, Benny saw the little girl. The principal was standing beside her.

"Good morning, everyone," the principal said.

After the class greeted the principal, she took the little girl's hand and led her into the classroom. She said, "This is Anika. She is an exchange student from a different country and she's here to join your class for a month."

Seeing a new face made everyone excited. Benny and the rest of his classmates smiled at the girl and she smiled back.

She waved at them and said, "Hello. I'm happy to be here. I hope we can all be great friends."

Ms. Molly showed Anika to her seat, then thanked the principal for helping the girl find their classroom. After that, Ms. Molly started with the day's lesson.

When it was time for recess, everyone quickly ran outside. Benny watched as Anika took out her snack box. He took his time in taking out his snack box too. The little boy took a deep breath and walked toward his new classmate.

"Hello, my name is Benny. I really like your hair," he said.

"Thank you! I really like my hair too," said Anika with a grin. "Everyone's excited about recess, huh? They just rushed outside!"

"It's their favorite part of the day," Benny said with a chuckle.

"What about you? Don't you like recess?" Anika asked.

"I do. But I do other things when it's recess. Instead of playing the whole time, I like to draw and daydream," Benny said shyly.

"That's awesome! I love daydreaming too. Have you ever tried daydreaming about the future and what you would like to be when you grow up?" Anika asked.

The little girl sat on her chair and opened her snack box. Benny did the same.

"Well..." Benny started.

"Well?" asked the little girl.

"You don't want to hear about my dream. It's... silly," he said.

"Why would you say that? Do you want to become a clown when you grow up?" asked Anika.

"What?! No!" exclaimed Benny while giggling.

Anika giggled too, then said, "There's nothing wrong with wanting to be a clown, of course. It's just the first thing that came to my mind when you said that your dream was silly."

Benny laughed out loud. Anika was very funny. She wasn't like his other classmates who didn't like to listen to him talk about his dreams.

The truth was, the little boy had a big dream. But when he shared his dream with his classmates, they laughed at him!

"We live in a small town, Benny," said his best friend.

"How can you possibly have a dream that big?" said another friend with a chuckle.

Since then, the little boy never talked about his dreams.

"So... Tell me!" Anika said while munching on an apple.

"Well... Why don't you tell me your dream first?" Benny asked.

"I'd love to!" Anika exclaimed. Then she stood up and twirled around, "When I grow up, I want to become a ballerina! I want to study in the best dance school and dance on the biggest stages around the world."

"Wow," Benny said.

"When I shared my dream with my classmates, they didn't believe I could do it. That made me sad. But when I told my teacher about it, she told me that I shouldn't be afraid to dream big!" Anika said cheerfully.

Benny smiled at his new friend.

The little girl sat back down and said, "I shared my dream, now what's yours?"

"When I grow up, I want to become an astronaut," he said shyly.

"That's so cool! I can just imagine you getting into a rocket and going to all the different planets. That's such an amazing dream, Benny," Anika said.

"Thanks. Even if I come from a small town, I really believe that I can become an astronaut. I'll study a lot and work hard until I reach my dream," he said.

"That's the spirit!" Anika said. "I'm glad you shared your dream with me, Benny. I believe in you. No matter what other people say, just keep your eyes on the prize and you will surely get where you want to be."

The little boy nodded. He was glad that Anika came to their class from another country. Benny almost gave up on his dream after his classmates made him feel like he couldn't make it.

When the recess bell rang once again, all the other children came back into the class. Benny stood up and went back to his seat while Anika packed her snack box away.

As Benny sat down, he had the biggest smile on his face. Having a friend like Anika who wasn't afraid to dream big was wonderful. After spending time with his new friend, the little boy felt like he could do anything!

Believing in Yourself

Go confidently in the direction of your dreams.
Live the life you have imagined.
– HENRY DAVID THOREAU

David was a little boy with a big family. He lived in a house with his dad, mom, three sisters, and four brothers. David was the youngest and he always wanted to do the same things his siblings were doing.

"Come on, guys! We're going to be late!" Ethan called out from the front door.

Ethan was the eldest child in David's family. He was calling his brothers as they were going to the park to play baseball with the other children in the neighborhood.

"I'm ready!" David said with a grin.

"Oh. I didn't know that you were coming," Ethan said.

"You left me here at home last time. You promised that I can come next time and that's today!" cried the little boy.

"That's right," Ethan said. "Just stay with us all the time, okay?"

David's three other brothers came running down the stairs. Then together, the five brothers left the house.

When they arrived at the park, David felt very excited. It was the first time that his brothers brought him along to play. All of his brothers loved to play baseball. So the little boy practiced throwing his baseball and swinging his bat every afternoon. He wanted to show his brothers that he was big enough to play with them.

"There you are! You're the only ones we were waiting for," said one of the boys from their neighborhood.

David saw that all the other boys were already in position. Ethan and the three other brothers joined their friends on the field.

The little boy ran after his big brother and asked, "Where should I stand?"

"Oh," said Ethan. He looked around and saw a group of little boys sitting on a bench near the edge of the park. "For now, go sit over there with

the other little boys. Watch us play first, then I'll call you when you can play."

"I know how to play baseball! I've been practicing at home," David said.

But Ethan wasn't listening. He was already running toward his friends in the middle of the park. With a sigh, the little boy walked toward the bench. He sat with the other little boys who weren't even watching the game.

"I know how to play baseball. I believe I can do it!" he said to himself.

David watched as his brothers had fun playing baseball with the other boys from the neighborhood. He kept waiting for Ethan or one of his other three brothers to call him over so that he could play too.

The little boy waited and waited until he drifted off to sleep.

"David! Wake up! It's time to go," said a voice that woke the little boy up.

David sat up and rubbed his eyes, "Is it my turn to play?"

"No, it's time to go home," Ethan said.

The little boy saw that it was already afternoon and everyone else was leaving. He felt bad because he didn't even get a chance to play.

"I thought you were going to call me," he said sadly.

"Well, we were all so busy. And when I looked over here, I saw that you were asleep," Ethan said. "Maybe next time."

"I know I can play. I've been practicing," David insisted.

"Okay, I promise to let you join next time," said his big brother.

Even though David was upset, he followed his big brother. Ethan caught up with the other three boys and they all started talking about the game.

David listened grumpily. He really believed that he could play baseball with the big boys. If only they would give him a chance.

When they arrived at their house, David's older brothers took turns in taking a bath. The sun was already setting, which meant that they would be having dinner in a while. Since he still felt upset, the little boy went outside. He sat on the doorstep. Watching people walk by made him feel calm.

David was so focused on his thoughts that he didn't hear the door open behind him. He also didn't notice when Dad sat down next to him.

"Are you alright, David?" Dad asked.

"Huh?" David said in surprise.

When he saw Dad, he asked, "When did you get here?"

"Just now," Dad said with a chuckle. "All of your brothers are talking about how much fun they had at the park. Why aren't you with them? Didn't you go to the park too?"

"I did. But I didn't get a chance to play," said the little boy sadly.

"Do you want to tell me what happened?" Dad asked gently.

David nodded. Then he told his dad what happened when they went to the park. He told his dad how he really wanted to play and how he believed he would do a great job. But his brothers never called him over to join the game.

After listening to David's story, Dad sighed and said, "No wonder you're feeling down. But you know, I also believe you would have played really well today."

"Really?" asked the little boy.

"Yes! I've seen how hard you've been practicing the past two weeks after school. I've been watching you from the kitchen window," Dad explained. "I'm proud of how hard you practiced. And I'm very happy to see how much you believe in yourself."

David smiled. Dad always knew the right thing to say whenever he was feeling down.

"Thanks, Dad," he said.

"You're welcome," Dad said as he ruffled the little boy's hair.

"Do you really think they will let me play next time as they promised?" he asked.

"I hope so," Dad said. "Even if they don't you should still keep trying to make yourself better. When you keep believing in yourself and you practice all the time, other people will also see how amazing you are."

"By other people, do you mean my brothers?" David asked.

"Your brothers and all the other boys from the neighborhood," Dad said. "I have always believed in you and seeing you practice made me believe in you even more."

"Thanks, Dad. And I promise that I will always believe in myself no matter what," said the little boy.

Now that David felt better, he went back inside the house with his dad to join the rest of the family for dinner.

Curious Caleb

The beautiful thing about learning is that
no one can take it away from you.
—B.B KING

aleb is a curious young boy who loved to ask questions. He lived in a small house with his mom. Caleb loved to learn new things and this made his mom very happy. Whenever he had a question to ask, his mom was always happy to answer.

"Good morning, Mom!" Caleb said cheerfully as he went into the dining room one morning.

"Good morning, Caleb," Mom answered with a smile. "I prepared your favorite breakfast because today is a special day."

"Really? Why is today so special?" asked the little boy.

"Did you forget already?" Mom asked with a giggle. "It's your first day of school!"

"Oh, right."

Caleb was excited to go to school. He just finished first grade and now, summer vacation was over. The little boy was excited to start second grade because he knew that he would learn a lot of new things.

"Maybe you would have remembered if we hadn't prepared your school things last week!" Mom said while chuckling.

The little boy was so excited to go to school that he begged his mom to help him prepare his school bag a week earlier. They bought all of his school supplies, placed names on all of his books, and even sharpened all of his pencils.

Then for the rest of the week, Mom and Caleb spend their days at parks, movie theaters, and malls. Mom wanted the little boy to relax and have fun before going back to school. The past week was so much fun that he forgot all about his first day.

"I think you're right, Mom!" Caleb exclaimed.

As Caleb and his mom enjoyed a delicious breakfast of pancakes, bacon, and blueberries, they talked about all the places they visited. While going to different places, the little boy asked so many questions!

While at the park, he asked how caterpillars became butterflies when he spotted a cocoon on one of the leaves of a plant.

While at the movie theater, he asked why they turned off all the lights when the movie started.

While at the mall, he asked how malls were built and who built them.

"I'm excited to learn a lot of new things. I hope my teacher will answer all of my questions," he said with a grin.

When they finished their meals, Mom tidied up while the little boy got dressed. Then the two of them left for school. Mom dropped Caleb off every morning before going to work. She didn't have to bring him to his classroom because he already knew where it was.

"See you after school," Mom said while waving goodbye.

"See you!" Caleb called out before running across the playground.

The little boy went straight to his classroom. He was excited to see his friends. He was excited to meet his new teacher too.

"Hi, guys!" he said cheerfully as he went inside the classroom.

"Hi, Caleb!" they answered.

The little boy joined his friends who were gathered in one corner of the classroom. They were all talking about their summer vacations. Caleb listened happily as his friends talked about visiting other countries, going to farms, and spending time with their families.

When it was his turn to share, Caleb talked about all the places he went to with his mom. Just as he finished talking, the school bell rang. The boys went to find their seats. Minutes later, the teacher came into the classroom.

"Good morning," she said.

"Good morning," said Caleb and the rest of the children in the classroom.

"Now that you are in second grade, I expect you to listen carefully. You are not little children anymore. I expect you to behave," she said sternly.

While the whole class was quiet, Caleb raised his hand.

"Yes?" asked the teacher while pointing to the little boy.

"May we know your name please?" he asked.

"My name is Ms. Agatha. Now sit down. The lesson is about to begin."

Instead of sitting down, Caleb asked what their lesson was going to be. He asked because he was excited.

"I said, sit down," Ms. Agatha replied.

The little boy did as he was told. Then Ms. Agatha started speaking. She talked about the solar system and all of the planets. Caleb got even more excited! Over the summer, he visited the Planetarium with his mom a couple of times.

After Ms. Agatha named all of the planets, Caleb raised his hand again.

"Yes?" asked the teacher while pointing to him.

"Are you going to tell us some cool facts about all of the planets?" he asked cheerfully.

"How can I when you keep raising your hand?" said Ms. Agatha with a frown. "From now on, nobody will ask questions until I am done!"

The smile disappeared from Caleb's face. Nobody has ever told him not to ask questions before. In fact, Mom always told him that asking a lot of questions was a good thing.

Ms. Agatha continued with the lesson while the whole class listened quietly. After she talked about the planets, she started talking about the sun. Caleb got excited once again that he forgot his teacher's rule.

The little boy raised his hand.

With a frown, Ms. Agatha said, "What is it now?"

"Can you tell us about all the other stars in our universe aside from the sun?"

Instead of answering his question, Ms. Agatha grunted. She told the little boy to sit down, then she continued to talk about the sun. To Caleb's dismay, she didn't even talk about the other stars.

After Ms. Agatha's class, Caleb didn't feel excited anymore. He kept thinking about how Ms. Agatha got upset because he asked a lot of questions. The little boy got lost in his thoughts that he wasn't able to listen to the other teachers.

When it was time to go home, the little boy's smile had disappeared completely. He waved goodbye to his friends and slowly walked out of the school.

"Caleb!" Mom called out with a smile.

But her smile went away too when she saw the little boy.

"What happened?"

With a sigh, Caleb told his mother about Ms. Agatha. He talked about how he asked her some questions and how she got upset each time he raised his hand.

"Was I wrong, Mom? Is it wrong to ask too many questions?" the little boy wondered.

"Of course, not!" Mom answered. "Maybe Ms. Agatha was just having a bad day. Or maybe she felt nervous about the first day of school too. There could be many reasons why your teacher acted that way. What about your other teachers? Did you try asking them a lot of questions too?"

"No. I kept thinking about what happened with Ms. Agatha that I didn't even notice my other teachers," he admitted.

"That's okay. You can always find out more about your other teachers tomorrow," Mom said.

"So... it's okay to keep asking questions?"

"Yes!" Mom exclaimed. "Don't be afraid to ask a lot of questions, especially if those questions will help you learn. I know how much you enjoy learning and I love that about you. Even if some

people don't answer your questions, you can always ask me."

Finally, Caleb smiled. He thanked his mom for being so awesome. As they walked home, the little boy's excitement came back. He wanted to learn more about his other teachers and ask them a lot of questions too.

I Can Do It!

Life is full of happiness and tears;
be strong and have faith.
—KAPOOR KHAN

iley was a friendly little boy. He lived in a small house with his mom, dad, and little sister, Rosie. Riley loved his little sister very much. He played with her every day and always made sure that she was safe.

While growing up, Riley's parents were both very busy. His dad spent all day at the office while his mom worked at home. So he often took care of his little sister.

"Play, Riley! Play!" exclaimed Rosie one afternoon while the little boy was doing his homework.

"Give me a few minutes, Rosie. I'll just finish my homework," he said.

"But I want to play now!" she said loudly.

When Riley didn't listen, the little girl climbed up on the couch. Then she started jumping up and down on it.

"Be careful, Rosie. You might fall!" Riley exclaimed.

He stood up in a hurry and ran to his little sister. Riley placed his hands around Rosie's waist and

lifted her up. The little boy planned to carry her off the couch and place her on the floor so she wouldn't fall down.

"Riley! What are you doing? You're not strong enough to carry your sister!" Mom cried out when she spotted the little boy.

"But she was jumping up and down the couch and I was just..."

Before he could finish talking, Mom took Rosie out of his hands. She carried her and asked if she was alright.

Then she looked at Riley and said, "I keep telling you, Riley. Don't try to carry your sister. You just aren't strong enough."

"Okay," said the little boy sadly.

He just wanted to help but he got in trouble for it. Still, he wasn't mad at his mom or Rosie. He knew that he was strong enough and one day, he would prove himself to everyone.

"I will show them that I'm strong enough to protect my little sister," he said to himself before going back to his homework.

That night, when Dad came home, Riley and Rosie ran to greet him. They both jumped in their dad's arms to give him hugs and kisses.

When Dad put them down, he said, "It's nice to be home. Riley, can you please help me carry all of the stuff I bought from the supermarket?"

"Sure!" exclaimed the little boy.

Dad always asked him for help with carrying things. It made the little boy very happy each time Dad asked for help.

"I got your favorite cookies and Rosie's favorite cereal. I also bought two flavors of ice cream for everyone to share. You can carry the bag with all of those treats, right?" Dad asked with a wink.

"Yes! Because I'm strong!" the little boy exclaimed.

He took the bag of groceries from his dad and carried it all the way to the kitchen. When he got there, he saw that mom was chopping some vegetables.

"Look, Mom. I helped Dad carry the groceries from the car," he said proudly.

"That's great, Riley. Just place the bag on the countertop. Thank you," she said without looking at the little boy.

With a sigh, Riley did as he was told. Then he asked Mom where his sister was. After finding out that she was in the living room, he went to find her.

"There you are," he said.

"Riley! Can we play now?" asked the little girl.

The little boy nodded, which made his sister cheer with delight. The two children played together until it was time for dinner. Then they ate together with their parents and prepared for bed.

Rosie begged Mom and Dad to let her sleep in Riley's room. She wanted him to tell her a bedtime story before going to sleep.

"Just promise that you will both go to sleep right after Riley's story," Mom said.

"We promise!" they answered.

Riley helped Rosie climb up on his bed as their parents left the room. Then he took a book from the shelf and sat down next to her. The little boy chose a book that he knew his little sister loved.

As he read the story, the little girl fell asleep. Before he could finish reading, Riley drifted off to sleep too.

The next morning, Riley woke up before his sister. It was Sunday morning, which meant that they didn't have to go to school. He hopped off the bed and got dressed. Then he brushed his teeth and went back to his room. When he got there, he saw Rosie sitting on his bed with a big smile on her face.

"Good morning!" she said.

"Good morning. You woke up just in time for breakfast. Go get dressed and brush your teeth. It's Sunday today, which means that..."

"We can go to the park!" exclaimed the little girl before Riley could finish his sentence.

Right away, Rosie jumped off Riley's bed and ran outside. The little boy chuckled while he started making his bed. When he was done, he went to the dining room. Mom was already there and breakfast was on the table.

Minutes later, Rosie ran into the dining room, and said, "I'm here! Good morning!"

Riley enjoyed breakfast with his family. The two children were very excited because their parents allowed them to play in the park every Sunday morning. The park was very close to their home so Mom and Dad didn't have to go with them.

After eating, the two children said goodbye to their parents.

They skipped and hopped all the way to the park. When they got there, they saw all of their friends.

Sunday morning was their favorite time of the week. They played all morning and had a delicious lunch prepared by their mom.

"Be careful, okay? Just call me if you need my help," Riley said before leaving his sister in the sandbox with her friends.

Then he ran to the other side of the park where his friends were playing. Everything was going well until Riley heard Rosie screaming loudly. The little boy stopped playing. He ran toward the sandbox where he left his little sister.

"Rosie!" he cried out while searching for her.

"She's up there," said a little boy who was sitting in the sandbox. He was pointing at the big slide.

Riley spotted his little sister. She was in the middle of the stairs going up to the slide. Her arms were wrapped around the railing and her eyes were shut tight. She was screaming loudly while some grown-ups were trying to pull her off the stairs.

The little boy ran toward the slide. When he got there, he called out to his sister.

"Rosie! Come down from there!"

"No! I'm s-scared," she stammered.

Riley knew that his little sister wouldn't let go when she felt scared. He knew that she wouldn't let anyone else carry her either. So he stepped towards her. The little boy stood on his tiptoes and placed his hands around her waist.

"You can let go now. I will carry you," he said gently.

Rosie let go of the railing and placed her arms around her big brother. Riley smiled and hugged his sister. When he turned around, he saw Mom and Dad standing behind them. They were both smiling.

"I should have listened when you said you were strong enough," Mom said.

"We're proud of you, Riley," said Dad.

"You're the best big brother ever!" exclaimed the little girl.

Riley felt wonderful. Now that he proved that he was strong enough, he promised to always be strong for himself and his little sister, Rosie.

The Brave Little Boy

When you have confidence, you can do anything.
—SLOANE STEPHENS

Vincent is a little boy who loved to go on adventures. He always dreamt of becoming an explorer when he grows up. But the little boy had a big problem... he was too scared to do anything!

"Mom! Guess what? We're going on a field trip to the Magical Caves next week," said Vincent's big brother, Vernon.

Mom just picked up the two brothers from school and she was driving them home. Vernon loved going on adventures too. But unlike Vincent, Vernon was very brave.

"How wonderful! According to the legends, there are magical creatures in those caves. And if you see one, they might grant you a wish," Mom said with a smile. "Will your class go to the Magical Caves too, Vincent?"

The little boy nodded. He wanted to visit the caves, but he was too scared. Going with his friends was even worse because he didn't want them to see how scared he was.

"Maybe you'll both see magical creatures when you visit!" Mom exclaimed cheerfully.

On their way home, Vernon talked about their field trip. He was very excited. He had been begging his parents to take him there for months. Vincent listened to his big brother talking about the caves excitedly.

He was so happy about their field trip that a smile came to Vincent's face too. Maybe he wouldn't get scared once he reached the caves. Maybe it wasn't too dark inside because the caves were magical. The more Vincent thought about it, the more excited he felt.

When they arrived home, Vincent started talking to his brother about the Magical Caves.

"Do you think it will be bright inside the caves?" he wondered.

"What do you mean?" asked Vernon.

"Well... since the caves are magical, maybe they won't be too dark inside. After all, the magical creatures inside wouldn't want to live in darkness, right?"

"I don't think I've ever heard of caves that aren't dark inside. Not even in movies! But that's part of the adventure, right? Exploring dark caves while trying to search for magical creatures sounds so awesome," said Vernon.

But Vincent didn't agree. His excitement disappeared and he went back to feeling scared. With a sigh, the little boy went to his room and sat on his bed.

"I wonder what I can say to Mom and Dad so they won't let me go," he said to himself.

For the next few days, Vincent tried to think of an excuse that would get him out of the field trip. But he couldn't think of anything. Before he knew it, the day of the field trip arrived.

"I'm so excited!" Vernon exclaimed as he went inside the school bus.

Vincent trailed behind his big brother. He didn't feel excited at all. He felt like there were

butterflies in his stomach. The little boy could feel his hands shaking too.

"Come on, Vincent. Mom told us to sit together, right?" Vernon reminded him.

Vincent nodded and did as he was told. Since the whole school was going on a field trip, siblings were allowed to ride the bus and explore the caves together. This made Vincent feel a little better.

When they arrived at the entrance of the magical caves, all of the children came out of the bus, including the two brothers. Without realizing it, Vincent grabbed his big brother's arm.

"Are you scared?" Vernon asked.

"N-no," he stammered.

Vernon shrugged and walked toward the caves. When they went inside, Vincent's heart pounded faster as everything went dark. Vernon was right. The caves were dark. Even though they were magical, there weren't any lights inside them.

While walking, the little boy suddenly stumbled. He didn't notice that his shoelaces had come undone and he stepped on them, which made him trip.

"Are you okay?" Vernon asked.

"Y-yes. Can you please wait for me while I tie my shoelaces?" Vincent asked.

"Let me just catch up to everyone else. I'll ask them to wait too," Vernon said.

As Vernon walked toward their schoolmates, the little boy knelt sat down and started tying his shoelaces. Just then, he heard a soft sound behind him. It sounded like soft footsteps.

Vincent turned around carefully. He hoped that it wasn't one of his classmates who would try to jump out of the darkness and scare him.

"Wh-who's there?" he stammered.

But he didn't need an answer when he turned around. The little boy's eyes widened in surprise when he saw a little person tiptoeing behind him.

"Uh-oh," said the tiny boy.

"Who... What are you?" Vincent asked softly.

"You saw me, huh?" he said with a sigh.

Then the tiny boy walked toward Vincent. He grinned at the little boy and bowed down. Vincent saw that the tiny boy had light green skin, bright green eyes, and curly brown hair. He had pointy ears too.

The tiny boy was wearing clothes that looked like they were made from dried leaves. He wasn't wearing any shoes.

"My name is Charlie, and I am an elf. I live inside these Magical Caves with all the other elves," he said.

"You're an elf? Wow!" Vincent exclaimed.

"Ssshhhh. Don't let the other children hear you."

"Oh, okay," Vincent said in a soft voice. "My name is Vincent. It's nice to meet you."

"It's nice to meet you too. So... what are you doing here?"

The little boy told the elf about his school's visit to the Magical Caves. He told the elf that they took field trips to visit new places and learn new things.

"I didn't even want to come but now, I'm glad I did, because I met you! A real elf," said the little boy.

"Why didn't you want to come?" Charlie asked.

"Well... I was scared. When I tried to imagine exploring dark caves, I felt scared. I'm not brave like my brother, Vernon," he admitted.

"But you still came even though you felt scared?"

Vincent nodded.

"Then that means you are brave!" said Charlie.

"What do you mean?" asked Vincent.

"Being brave doesn't mean that you aren't scared of anything. It means doing something even if you're scared. When you joined your brother and schoolmates even though you were scared of exploring the dark caves, that showed how brave you truly are," Charlie explained.

"Really?"

Charlie nodded. Vincent wanted to ask more questions, but he heard footsteps coming toward him.

"That must be Vernon," he said.

"That's my cue to go," Charlie said. "And remember, you are brave. As long as you keep facing your fears even if you feel scared, that shows how brave you are."

"Thank you, Charlie," Vincent said.

The little elf clapped twice and disappeared. Vincent smiled. He was glad that he decided to join the field trip. He made a new magical friend and he discovered that he was a brave little boy after all.

The School Talent Competition

When you have confidence, you can
have a lot of fun. And when you have fun,
you can do amazing things.

—JOE NAMATH

Joshua was a little boy who loved to dance. Ever since he was young, he would move his body to the beat whenever he heard some music. When he reached second grade, he had become so good at dancing that his parents always encouraged him to join competitions.

"I'm not good enough to compete, Mom," he always said.

But Mom and Dad believed in Joshua. They hoped that one day, the little boy would find the confidence to show the world what a talented dancer he was.

One morning, when Joshua went to school, he noticed something different. The halls were empty and he heard a strange noise coming from the auditorium. The little boy rushed to the auditorium to see what was going on.

"I can't believe it!" said someone excitedly when Joshua entered the auditorium.

"Do you think anyone can join?" someone asked.

Joshua wondered what they were talking about. He walked around the room until he saw some of his classmates. They were standing together near the corner of the auditorium with their teacher, Ms. Ashley.

"Hey, guys. What's going on?" he asked.

"The principal just told us about a very special talent competition that will happen in a month," one of his classmates replied.

Joshua wondered what the big deal was. They always had talent competitions at school. But this time, the whole school gathered in one place to hear about it.

"He didn't tell you the exciting part," said Joshua's best friend, Avery.

"I knew I was missing something."

"The student who wins the talent competition will win tickets for a tour of the ten best amusement parks around the country for their whole family," Avery explained.

"Whoa!" Joshua exclaimed. "No wonder everyone's excited."

"Everyone wants to join, but only one student from each class will be chosen to compete," Avery explained.

"Only one?" Joshua asked.

When he first heard about the competition, he felt excited. He knew that he was a good dancer and for a moment, he thought about joining. But when he found out that only one student per class would compete, he didn't think he was good enough.

"Okay, everyone. You can go back to your classrooms," the principal announced. "If you have any questions or you want to sign up for the audition at the end of the week, you can ask your teachers."

Joshua followed his teacher and classmates back to the classroom. When they arrived and everyone went to their seats, Joshua's classmates started asking Ms. Ashley lots of questions about the talent competition.

"Alright, everyone. I know you're all excited. Please settle down and I will explain everything," she said.

As the whole class went silent, Ms. Ashley said, "A group of very special people has seen how wonderful our school is, which is why they wanted to reward us with something amazing.

"They decided to hold a talent competition to encourage you and everyone else in the school to confidently show your talents. But having everyone perform at the talent competition would take too much time. That's why they asked us to choose just one student per class."

"But how will you choose which student will join from our class?" asked one of Joshua's classmates.

"We will have an audition by the end of the week. Anyone can try it out. Before going home, tell me if you want to join the audition and I'll sign you up," said the teacher. "All of the teachers will be the judges for the audition and by next week, we will announce the names of the children who will join the final talent competition."

After explaining, Ms. Ashley started the lesson for the day. But Joshua wasn't listening. While his teacher talked, the little boy thought about the talent competition. He thought about dancing on stage in front of the whole school.

He also thought about what it would feel like to win the competition. The little boy knew that his family would be super excited if he won the prize. He also knew that his parents would be very happy just by joining.

Joshua was so distracted the whole day that he didn't understand.

"Joshua, may I talk to you for a moment?" Ms. Ashley said just as the little boy was about to leave the classroom.

The little boy walked toward his teacher and asked, "Did I do something wrong?"

Ms. Ashley smiled at him warmly, "I noticed that you were a bit distracted after I talked about the talent competition. I know that you're an amazing dancer. I was hoping you would join the audition."

"Oh... Um... I-I don't know," he said. "I don't think my dancing is good enough."

"Why don't you think about it and tell me tomorrow?" Ms. Ashley suggested.

Joshua nodded and thanked his teacher. When he went home, he was still thinking about the competition. He wanted to dance but he didn't feel confident enough.

"Are you okay, Joshua?" Mom asked while walking home.

Every afternoon, Mom picked Joshua off from school and they walked home together. Joshua usually talked a lot while walking home, but he was very quiet that day.

At first, Joshua didn't want to tell his mom about the competition. But she kept asking, so he told her about it.

"That sounds wonderful, Joshua! Will you give it a try?"

"I don't know. I don't think my dancing is better than the talents of my classmates," he said.

"I see," Mom said. "Well, whether you join or not, we will always be proud of you. Dad and I are your biggest fans and to us, your dancing is the best talent in the world!"

Joshua smiled at his mom and hugged her. They just arrived at their house and the little boy went straight to his room.

He sat on his bed and said to himself, "Maybe it's time for me to show off my talent."

After a while, the little boy drifted off to sleep. When he woke up, he felt hungry. So he went to the kitchen to find something to eat. Just as he was about to go into the kitchen, he heard his parents talking.

"I wish Joshua would join the talent competition. He's an amazing dancer. He is very confident when talking in front of other people and joining quiz bees. But when it comes to his dancing, he just doesn't believe in himself enough," Mom said.

"You're right. Ever since he was a toddler, Joshua was an incredible dancer. Even if he doesn't win the competition, I'm sure everyone will love his performance," Dad said. "Still, I know he will win if he joins."

Joshua suddenly felt happy. His parents didn't know that he could hear them talking. And yet, they still had wonderful things to say about his special talent. They believed in him so much that it gave him the confidence to try out for the audition.

With a deep breath, the little boy went into the kitchen to tell his parents the good news. Joshua finally found his confidence and he was ready to show everyone how amazing he was!

The Broken Vase

The time is always right to do what is right.
—MARTIN LUTHER KING, JR.

Eugene was a little boy with a very special secret. He lived in a small house with his dad, mom, and little brother. Their house was surrounded by a garden and in that garden lived a little fairy named Mandy.

Mandy was Eugene's friend.

He met the little fairy when he was just four years old. One night, the little boy went outside because he thought he saw a firefly flying outside the window. Eugene loved fireflies!

Eugene ran outside excitedly and slipped on the doormat. He started crying and calling out to his parents. But Dad was in the toilet and Mom was preparing dinner. Neither of them heard him crying.

To his surprise, the little firefly flew closer to him. The firefly flew right in front of the little boy's face and said, "Are you okay?"

That's when Eugene realized that the firefly wasn't a firefly at all. It was a fairy!

"Ouchie," he said while sniffling.

The little fairy flew all around Eugene to check where he was hurt. She saw that he skinned his knee. The fairy landed on Eugene's knee and gently blew on his wound. Right away, the pain disappeared and so did Eugene's injury.

"No more ouchie," he said as he wiped away his tears.

"My name is Mandy and I live in your beautiful garden," said the fairy.

"My name is Eugene," the little boy said with a smile.

Since then, Eugene and Mandy became very good friends. Now that the little boy was six years old, he was still friends with the little fairy who lived in their garden.

"Mandy, where are you?" Eugene called out softly one morning.

Moments later, the little fairy flew out of the bushes and went straight to Eugene. She smiled and waved at her friend.

"Hi! Have you eaten breakfast?" he asked.

"Good morning, Eugene! Yes, I have. I ate a few blueberries and drank some honey," she answered.

"Do you want to play with me today?"

"Of course!" exclaimed the little fairy.

Eugene and Mandy played together at the back of the house. Each time they played, they did it in the garden behind the little boy's house. Mandy was very shy. She didn't want other people to see her. So she asked Eugene to keep their friendship a secret.

"Check this out, Mandy. My friends and I have been practicing our cartwheels. I've gotten really good," he said proudly.

The little boy did one cartwheel on the grass while his fairy friend watched with delight. She giggled happily when Eugene completed his cartwheel.

"Amazing!" she exclaimed.

"We practiced every recess time this whole week. I couldn't wait to show you," said the little boy with a grin.

"I will learn a trick too and show you next week," said Mandy.

"Okay!"

Then the two friends continued to play. After a while, Mom came out of the house. Mandy flew into the bushes to hide while the little boy ran up to his mom.

"You just love playing here, don't you?" Mom asked.

"Yes! But what are you doing here?"

Mom held up a beautiful vase for the little boy to see. She painted vases and other house decorations, then sold them to other people. It was his mom's job.

"I just finished painting this vase and I want to put it out here to dry," Mom explained. "Please be careful while you play out here, okay?"

Eugene nodded and went to the bushes while Mom went back inside the house.

"Mom just wanted to leave one of her vases out here to dry," he whispered to his fairy friend.

"There's a new vase? I want to see it!"

Mandy loved Mom's paintings. She thought that Eugene's mom was very good at her job. She flew toward the vase and stopped right in front of it. The little fairy sighed and said that it was beautiful.

"I wish your mom could teach me how to paint too," she said.

"We can ask her," Eugene suggested.

"Oh, no. You know that I don't want other people to see me," she said shyly.

"But why?"

"Fairies shouldn't be seen by people because not all people are good. Some of them might start hunting us. I know your family isn't like that, but I'm too shy," she explained.

Eugene shrugged, then started doing cartwheels around the vase.

"Maybe you shouldn't do that too close to Mom's new vase," Mandy said.

But the little boy didn't listen. He did three cartwheels, lost his balance, and fell right on top of the vase! The vase cracked underneath Eugene, then it broke into tiny pieces.

"Oh, no," Eugene said.

"Are you okay?" Mandy asked worriedly.

The little boy nodded, "I'm fine. But Mom will be mad at me."

"What are you going to do?"

The little boy thought about it for a while. He looked around and wondered if Mom would believe him if he told her that the wind blew the vase over and it fell. But then, he noticed that there wasn't any wind blowing.

Just then, he had a great idea. He turned to Mandy and said, "Wait for me here. I'll bring Ethan out

and tell Mom that he broke the vase. She won't be mad at him because he's just a toddler. And he won't tell on me because he can't even talk yet!"

"You want to blame your little brother for breaking the vase?" Mandy asked.

When Eugene nodded, she said, "But that's not right. You should be honest and tell Mom what happened. Don't you think she will be more upset if she finds out that you didn't tell her the truth?"

"But she won't find out! Nobody saw me break the vase and Ethan won't tell," said the little boy.

Mandy frowned, "But will you feel good about lying to your mom and blaming your little brother who didn't do anything wrong?"

Instead of answering, the little boy went inside the house. Moments later, he came back outside with his little brother, Ethan. He asked Ethan to sit on the grass next to the broken vase.

"See? Doesn't it look like he did it?" Eugene asked Mandy.

The little fairy sighed and shook her head. Then she flew toward the bushes just as Mom came outside.

When she saw the vase, Mom's eyes widened, and she asked, "What happened?"

"Well..." Eugene started.

He had a story ready, but he remembered how sad Mandy looked when he told her that he wouldn't tell Mom the truth. When he looked at Ethan, he saw that his little brother was smiling happily.

"I broke it," he admitted. "I was doing cartwheels and I fell on the vase. I'm sorry, Mom."

"Are you okay?" Mom asked.

Eugene was surprised. He thought that Mom would scold him.

"Yes. But... Aren't you mad?"

"Well, I am upset that you broke my vase. But I'm glad that you aren't hurt. More importantly, I'm proud of you for telling the truth. Now let's go inside and clean you up."

Eugene nodded and followed his mom. After cleaning up, he wanted to go back outside and thank Mandy for teaching him the importance of being honest.

Taking Responsibility

The price of greatness is responsibility.
—WINSTON CHURCHILL

Nolan was a little boy who loved animals. He lived in a house with his dad and mom. Since he was young, the little boy slept in the same room as his parents. But he was about to turn five in two weeks and was promised that he would get his own room.

"Have you thought about what you want for your birthday?" Mom asked one morning over breakfast.

"I know exactly what I want, Mom," answered the little boy with a smile.

"Oh? What is it?" Dad asked.

Mom and Dad have been asking Nolan what he wanted for his birthday for the past few weeks. But the little boy never had an answer for them. Now that he did have an answer, both parents were curious.

"I would like to have my own pet. A pet that can keep me company when I get my own room," he said.

Nolan's parents weren't surprised by the little boy's birthday wish. Ever since he was young, he loved animals! His love of animals started when they took him to the zoo a few years ago.

For his second birthday, Mom and Dad planned a trip to the zoo with Nolan. The little boy was amazed at all of the animals in the zoo. He giggled in delight when the animals looked at him. And he was able to remember all of their names after they spent the whole day exploring.

Since then, Nolan became a real fan of animals.

His school things had pictures of animals on them, his clothes had animal prints, and he loved drawing different kinds of animals too. So when he asked for a pet, Mom and Dad weren't too surprised.

"Can you let Dad and I talk about it first?" Mom asked.

"Okay," said the little boy.

Mom wanted to give Nolan his birthday wish. But she was a bit worried because Nolan wasn't very responsible. He left messes everywhere he went, he forgot things all the time, and he got bored with toys easily.

She was worried that the little boy might not take care of a pet well if they got him one. During the first few weeks, he might be able to look after his pet. But since he hasn't learned how to be responsible yet, Mom was worried that having a pet would be too much for him.

Mom wanted to explain this to Dad after Nolan finished eating. The little boy excused himself and went to the living room to play.

"So what kind of pet should we get for Nolan?" Dad asked.

"I don't know. Do you think it's a good idea?' Mom wondered.

"What do you mean?"

"He's just five years old and he hasn't learned how to be responsible yet. After a few weeks, you or I might end up taking responsibility for Nolan's pet. But you go to work every day and I have to work here at home too. We can't just get a pet and not have a plan to take care of it. Having a pet is a big responsibility," Mom explained.

"Oh... You're right," Dad agreed.

Mom and Dad thought about what to do. They wanted to give Nolan his birthday wish. But at the same time, they wanted to make sure that he will take good care of his pet.

"Actually, this could be a good learning experience for him," Dad said.

"What do you mean?"

"We can explain to Nolan that owning a pet is a big responsibility. He needs to promise that he will take care of his pet and not pass that responsibility to us after a few weeks," Dad said.

"You're right. I have an idea too," Mom said.

She shared her idea with Dad and he agreed with it. While Mom washed the dishes, Dad went to the living room to talk to Nolan.

"Did you talk about it? Will you get me a pet for my birthday?" asked the little boy excitedly.

Dad sat next to the little boy. He talked about how important it was to take good care of a pet, "You need to feed your pet regularly, bathe it when needed, and do everything else needed to keep your pet happy and healthy."

"I know that, Dad."

"And you have to do that for as long as your pet is around. You can't just ask your mom or me to take care of your pet after a few weeks because you've grown bored of it. Mom and I have to work. We don't have time to take care of a pet," he explained.

"I can do it, Dad!"

"Okay. Let me give you a test. If you can show me that you're responsible in the next few days, Mom and I will grant your birthday wish," Dad promised.

"How do I show you that I'm responsible?" asked the little boy.

"You can start by helping out here at home. Tidy up your toys after playing, brush your teeth, and prepare for bed before Mom and I ask you to and check if you have homework when you come

home from school. Doing things like those without waiting for Mom and me to tell you shows that you're being responsible," said Dad.

"Okay. I'll show you how responsible I can be," the little boy said confidently.

And Nolan did just that. For the next few days, he showed his parents that he could be responsible. When he came home from school, he opened his bag to check if he had homework. After playing, he kept his toys in the correct places.

After reading books, he placed them back on the bookshelf. And when they finished eating dinner, he brushed his teeth and wore his pajamas without waiting for his parents to tell him.

All of the things Nolan did make his parents proud. They saw how hard the little boy worked to show them that he was responsible enough to have a pet.

By the end of the week, Mom and Dad asked Nolan to sit with them in the living room. Before joining them, the little boy kept all the toys that he was playing with when his parents called him.

"Why did you call me?" Nolan asked.

Mom and Dad both smiled at the little boy. They told him how happy and proud they were of everything he had done in the past few days.

"Dad and I have decided that you are responsible enough to have your own pet," Mom said.

"Really? Thank you!" exclaimed Nolan.

"But we have one last challenge for you. Are you ready for it?" Dad asked.

"I'm ready for anything!"

Mom and Dad asked Nolan to follow them to the extra bedroom. When they opened the door, Nolan was surprised to see that it was completely empty.

"Where did all of the stuff go?" he asked.

"We kept some stuff in our room and the rest of the stuff in the garage. Now, we all need to work together to prepare this room for you and your new pet," explained Mom.

"A new pet and a new room?! You're awesome!" the little boy said as he hugged his parents.

For the next few days, Mom, Dad, and Nolan fixed up his room. They decorated the walls, moved all of Nolan's things from his parent's bedroom to the new room, and added many other things to Nolan's bedroom.

"It's perfect," Nolan said when they were done.

"Now that your room is ready, it's time to make an important decision," Dad said.

"What decision?" asked the little boy.

"It's time to decide what kind of pet you want to get," said Mom.

"A turtle!" exclaimed Nolan.

Mom and Dad were surprised. They thought that it would take some time for Nolan to decide what pet to get from the pet shop. But he already knew what he wanted.

"My teacher has a pet turtle too. She keeps talking about it at school. She said that taking care of a turtle was a lot of fun. So I want a turtle too."

"Are you sure?" Mom asked.

"Yes! I even asked my teacher how to take care of a turtle," Nolan said.

Then the little boy talked about all of the tips his teacher shared with him about taking care of a pet turtle. Mom and Dad were impressed at how much Nolan had learned from his teacher. They had no idea that he already learned on his own.

"How responsible of you to ask your teacher to help you learn how to take care of a turtle," Mom said proudly.

"Well, I guess all that's left to do is to go to the pet store," Dad said.

"We can introduce your pet to everyone at your birthday party. I'm sure everyone will be excited to meet your new pet," Mom said.

Nolan felt very happy while he walked to the pet shop with his parents. He was about to get his birthday wish because he showed his parents just how responsible he could be.

The Strength Inside

The spirit of hope, inner strength,
enthusiasm and persistent determination
are the pillars for any success.
—LAILAH GIFTY AKITA

Peter was a little boy who lived in a little town. Tiny as he was, he lived in the biggest house in town with his mom, dad, and lots of nannies.

When Peter was younger, he lived in a tiny house. But his parents worked very hard to give their son a better life.

When Peter turned four, his parents started working a lot. So they hired a bunch of nannies to take care of the little boy. Peter missed his parents, but deep inside, he knew why they weren't around all the time.

"Good morning, Peter," said Nanny Tina, Peter's personal nanny.

"Good morning, Nanny Tina. Are Mom and Dad here today?" he asked.

"They will be home this evening," Nanny Tina said with a smile.

"Wow! I'm so excited!" Peter said cheerfully.

He thanked Nanny Tina for preparing his breakfast, then asked her to join him. While they ate a delicious breakfast of waffles and fresh fruits, Nanny Tina talked to Peter about the things he would do for the day.

It was going to be another busy day for Peter. He had school, violin lessons, swimming lessons, and even a baking class. The little boy loved to bake. When he was just three, his mom always asked him to bake with her every time she made cakes or cookies.

Now that Mom was too busy, she signed him up for a baking class for kids. It was Peter's favorite class ever!

After breakfast, Peter and Nanny Tina left for school. They rode in Peter's car and the driver brought them to school. While on the way, the little boy looked out the window. He wondered when he would be able to go to school with his parents again.

"We're here," Nanny Tina said.

Peter got so lost in his thoughts that he didn't notice that they had already arrived at school. He thanked the driver and his nanny for dropping him off, then he went inside the school.

The little boy ran straight to his classroom where his friends were waiting for him.

"Hi, Peter!" they said as they waved to the little boy.

"Hello," he said with a smile.

The little boy was so kind and friendly that everyone in his classroom loved him. He joined the group of children who were gathered in the middle of the room. They were talking about different things.

Peter liked listening to his friends. They all had different kinds of families and it was fun to hear about the times they spent with each other. Since Peter's parents were often away, he couldn't share many stories. Still, he enjoyed listening to his friends talk.

When the bell rang, Peter went to his seat. He listened attentively to his teacher and joined all of the activities they had in class. When the class was over, Peter said goodbye to his friends.

Outside, Nanny Tina was waiting for him. She waved at the little boy and he waved back as he walked toward her.

"How was school?" she asked.

"School was fine," he answered.

Then they hopped in the car to go to the little boy's next classes. First, Peter went to the mall. There was a shop at the mall that sold musical instruments and offered classes for children to learn how to play different musical instruments.

Nanny Tina waited for Peter outside the shop as he learned how to play the violin. When he was done, they went to the sports center for Peter to have his swimming lesson. Nanny Tina walked around the pool while Peter swam in the water.

Even though there were lifeguards in the pool area, Nanny Tina wanted to make sure that the little boy was safe. After his swimming lesson, Nanny Tina helped the little boy get dressed for his next, and favorite, class.

"Are you feeling okay?" she asked.

"Yes, Nanny Tina," he answered.

"Do you want to rest for a while or have a snack?"

"No, thank you. I have my baking class next. I don't want to be late. Our teacher will show us how to bake cupcakes today. That's Mom's favorite and I want to surprise her when she gets home," he said.

When they reached the school where Peter had his baking class, Nanny Tina waited in the lobby. The little boy waved goodbye and went to his classroom. Once there, he saw the other children in the class.

They were all talking to each other, except for one little girl who just sat in the corner. Peter knew the little girl, she lived in the house next to his.

"Hi, Adriana. Are you okay?" he asked.

The little girl looked up and sighed. Then she shook her head.

"What happened?"

"My mom and dad went out of town last week and they promised to be home today. But they said that they won't come home until next week," she said sadly.

Peter smiled at Adriana and said, "I know how you feel. My parents are always away. They have to work, you see. Sometimes, I don't see them for weeks."

"Really?"

When the little boy nodded, Adriana asked, "Don't you feel sad?"

"Sometimes, I do. But then I remember that they're doing everything for my future. And whenever they come home, they take me to fun places like amusement parks, the mall, and the zoo."

Adriana sighed. Peter wanted to make her feel better, but their teacher came into the room and the class started. While they learned how to bake cupcakes, the little boy kept looking at his friend who was working across the room.

While they waited for their cupcakes to bake in the oven, Peter had a great idea. He walked over to Adriana and asked her if she wanted to have a sleepover.

"I don't know. I should ask my parents first," she said.

"Okay. Why don't you talk to your nanny now? Maybe she can call your mom or dad for you," Peter suggested.

The little girl asked to be excused for a while so she could talk to her nanny. When she came back, she was smiling.

"Mom agreed since we just live next door. Nanny will bring me home after class so she can pack my bag, then she'll drop me off at your house," she said.

"That's great!" Peter exclaimed.

The sound of the oven timer meant that their cupcakes were ready. The teacher helped Peter, Adriana, and the rest of the children place their cupcakes in boxes. Then they all went home carrying their freshly-baked cupcakes.

"Nanny Tina, Adriana will sleep over at our house tonight," Peter said while handing his cupcake to her.

"I know. Adriana's nanny talked to me. We'll wait for her at home."

On their way home, Peter felt excited. It had been a while since one of his friends slept over. He got dressed and waited for his friend in the living room, which was next to the front door.

When the doorbell rang, Peter opened it excitedly.

"Hi, Adriana! Welcome," he said.

"Thanks for inviting me over. I feel better already," she said.

While playing, Adriana was amazed at Peter's inner strength. She thought Peter was only pretending to be okay with his parents being away all the time. But while they played together, she noticed that he was truly happy.

That afternoon, Adriana realized that she didn't have to be sad all the time when her parents were away. Just like Peter, she wanted to be happy by finding her own inner strength.

Kindness Matters

Be kind whenever possible. It is always possible.
—DALAI LAMA

William was a little boy with a big imagination. He was cheerful and friendly, and he loved to make new friends. The little boy lived with his Dad in a house right in the middle of a quiet neighborhood.

Behind their house was a small forest. It was filled with beautiful trees and lots of bushes with colorful fruits and flowers. Many people believed that it was a magical forest and that some enchanted creatures lived there.

"Do you think I will ever meet an enchanted creature, Dad?" William asked one morning.

William and his dad were in the backyard. Dad was planting some vegetables while William played around with the crops. While playing, the little boy kept looking at the forest. He had never been in the forest because Dad never allowed him to go there.

Dad stopped planting for a moment to look at his son. He said, "There have been stories of people spotting some enchanted creatures in that forest. But I don't think anyone has ever met one of those creatures."

"Maybe I'll be the first one!"

"Well, you never know," Dad said with a chuckle as he went back to planting.

"May I go into the forest, Dad? I won't go all the way in. I'll just walk around the edge where you can see me," said the little boy.

Dad stopped and looked up once again. William had been asking him to explore the forest for a long time now. He decided to allow the little boy.

"Okay. Just stay where I can see you. And when I'm done planting, we'll go back inside the house," he said.

"Thanks, Dad!" exclaimed the little boy.

He ran toward the forest and stopped right in front of the line of trees. Now that he was standing in front of the forest, he saw that it was quite dark inside. William looked up and saw that the leaves of the tall trees were covering the sky. No wonder it was dark in the forest.

Bravely, the little boy walked past the line of trees. He was surprised when he smelled something sweet. He didn't know where the sweet smell was coming from, but he liked it. The little boy walked around carefully.

He heard some birds chirping above the trees. The only other sound he heard was the sound of his footsteps.

Just then, he heard another soft sound coming from behind one of the bushes. It sounded like someone crying.

"H-hello?" he called out softly. "Is someone there?"

Nobody answered, but the crying sound continued. William's eyes grew wide when he realized that someone might need his help. He looked back toward their house and saw his dad busily planting in the garden.

William took a deep breath and walked toward the bush where the sound was coming from. With his right hand, he gently pushed the leaves aside. To his surprise, he saw a tiny animal on the ground.

It wasn't like any animal that William had ever seen before. It looked like a tiny puppy, but instead of fur, it had feathers! The little creature looked up at William and started crying. The sound was coming from it!

"Oh, no. Are you hurt?" he asked.

The little boy knelt down and gently picked up the little creature. It was very light and it smelled sweet, just like the forest.

"What... are you?" he asked.

Instead of answering, the little creature started crying again. William saw tears coming out from the little creature's eyes. William turned the little creature all around his hands gently to check if it was hurt.

But he didn't see any wounds on the creature.

"You don't seem to be hurt. Are you hungry?" he asked.

This time, the creature stopped crying. To William's surprise, it looked at him, and nodded!

"You can understand me!" he exclaimed. "Oh, and you're hungry. But what do you eat?"

The little boy looked at the bush where he found the creature. The top of the bush was full of sparkly golden berries. He wondered if the little creature was trying to get those berries.

William picked a few berries and offered them to the little creature. The little boy smiled as the creature gobbled up the berries in an instant. Then in giggled and jumped around on his palm.

"You like those, huh? Let me get some more for you."

William picked more berries and fed them to the little creature. Once again, it gobbled up the berries and giggled with delight. The little boy kept feeding berries to the creature until it gave a loud burp!

Just then, William heard footsteps walking toward him. He looked up and saw a scruffy-looking boy. He was short, his clothes were dirty and torn in places, and he had messy hair. The strange thing was that he had very big hands and feet.

"There you are!" exclaimed the boy.

"Me?" William asked.

"What?" asked the boy as he looked up at William. "Oh. Who are you and why are you holding my pet?"

"Your pet?"

"Yes, that's my pet you're holding. I've been looking for him everywhere!" he exclaimed.

"I'm sorry. I didn't know that this little creature was your pet. I found him behind that bush. He was crying so I fed him some berries," William explained.

"Oh... Thank you," said the boy.

"You're welcome. My name is William," he said while handing the creature to the boy.

The little creature looked even smaller in the boy's big hands. He said, "My name is Koduh. You're a human, right?"

"Yes. Aren't you a human too?"

The boy chuckled, "No, I'm not. I'm a forest troll."

"Wow. Does that mean that you live here?"

The troll nodded. He told William that there were many trolls in the forest, but they spent most of their days in the deep, dark part of the forest where humans don't go.

"I just came here looking for this little guy," he said. "Thanks again for feeding him. You're very kind. My mom said that humans don't really care about the creatures in the forest. But when you heard my pet crying, you picked him up, and fed him."

"Well... he sounded so sad," William said shyly.

"When I go home, I'll tell my mom and dad that there are some humans who are kind and I just met one," said Koduh with a grin.

Even though the troll had crooked teeth, William liked his smile. It was a very warm and friendly smile. The little boy also felt happy because he met an enchanted creature in the forest!

"Well, I have to go back now. My parents must be looking for me. And if they find out that I came here without their permission, I'll be in trouble," said the troll.

"Will I see you again?" William asked.

"Sure! I just need to ask permission so my parents know where I am."

Then the troll waved goodbye and walked into the forest. William smiled as he watched his new friend walk away. He was glad to have made a new friend.

Thanks to William's kindness, he was the first person to meet an enchanted creature in the magical forest. He couldn't wait to tell his dad all about it!

Do You Feel
What I Feel?

*You can only understand
people if you feel them in yourself.*
—John Steinbeck

Martin was a young boy with a big family. He was the middle child with two older sisters and two younger brothers. The little boy got along well with his sisters, but not with his brothers. The three little boys often got into fights with each other.

One afternoon, Martin's dad came home with a big bag of toys. He had just come home from a trip out of town and he had surprises for everyone. The five children lined up and got their toys from Dad. They were all excited.

Kayla, the eldest sister, got a new cooking set. Anika, the second sister, got two new stuffed toys. Martin got a remote-control car while his two younger brothers got some new dinosaur toys. Dad knew exactly what each of them wanted.

"Thank you, Dad!" said the children before going into the living room to play with their new toys.

Martin was very happy with his gift. His best friend, Nelson, had a remote-control car too. One day, he brought the car to school and let Martin play with it. Since then, the little boy had been asking his dad for a remote-control car too.

Nathaniel and Dennis, Martin's younger brothers, were busy playing with their new dinosaur toys. They didn't notice their big brother playing with his remote-control car. He let his car zoom all around the room before moving to the kitchen, the dining room, and his bedroom.

Martin loved his new toy. He also felt extra excited to tell his best friend that he had a remote-control car too. Martin and his siblings spend the rest of the day playing with their new toys.

They only stopped to have dinner together, then they all went to bed. Martin placed his new toy on his bed, then he kept the remote right next to it. That night, the little boy fell asleep with a smile on his face.

The next morning, Martin went to school with his older sisters. Nathaniel and Dennis didn't have school that day, so they stayed home with Mom. When Martin arrived at school, he rushed to the classroom to find Nelson.

"Hi, Martin," Nelson said.

"Hey! You'll never guess what Dad gave me yesterday," he said with a grin.

"What?"

"A remote-control car! It's just like the one you have! Now, we can play with our cars together!" said the little boy excitedly.

"Cool! Why don't you come over after school and bring your car? We can play in our backyard," Nelson said.

Martin agreed with his best friend's great plan. The little boy was so excited that he only thought about playing with Nelson for the rest of the day. When it was time to go home, Martin walked with his best friend.

Nelson's house was right next to Martin's. When they reached Nelson's house, Martin waved good-bye to his best friend.

"I'll just get my toy car and ask permission from Mom. I'll be back right away," he said.

The little boy ran toward his house. He opened the door and rushed to his room. But when he got there, he didn't see his precious new toy on his bed.

"Where is it?" he asked out loud.

Martin searched for his toy all over his room, but he couldn't find it. Then he went to the living room to search, but it wasn't there either. With tears in his eyes, Martin went looking for his mom.

"Mom!" he called out.

"I'm in the kitchen," she answered.

The little boy went to the kitchen. When he got there, he saw his mom setting the table.

"Mom, did you see my new toy? The one Dad gave me yesterday," he said.

"Which one was your toy? The dinosaurs or the remote-control car?" she asked.

"The car."

"Oh. I think Nathaniel and Dennis took the car outside. A while ago, they asked me if it was okay to play in the backyard," Mom said.

"What? But that's my toy, Mom!" Martin said in a loud voice.

Before Mom could say anything, the little boy ran out of the kitchen. He went straight to the back-yard where he saw his brothers playing happily with his new toy. Nathaniel was controlling the car with the remote while Dennis was running after the car. It looked like he was trying to catch it.

"Hey! You two! Give me back my toy!" he yelled.

Nathaniel got so startled by Martin's loud voice that he dropped the remote control. The remote control fell to the ground and broke.

"Uh oh," Nathaniel said with wide eyes.

Dennis stopped running when the car stopped moving. He looked up at his brother with wide eyes too. He picked up the car and walked toward his two older brothers. The little boy looked scared.

"Oh, no!" cried Martin. "Look at what you did! You broke my toy!"

"I'm s-sorry," Nathaniel said as tears fell down his cheeks. "I got startled when you yelled at me."

Martin picked up the broken pieces of his remote control, then grabbed the car from Dennis who started crying too.

"I'm sorry too. We just wanted to play with your car because it's so cool," Dennis said while sniffling.

"You two are the worst brothers in the world!" Martin exclaimed before stomping off.

Feeling upset, the little boy stomped all the way to Nelson's house. When he got there, he saw his best friend in the front yard, waiting for him.

"There you are! What took you so long?" Nelson asked.

Martin showed Nelson his broken remote control. Then he told his best friend what happened.

Nelson smiled at Martin as he took the remote control. He placed the batteries back inside, then closed them up. Nelson took the car from Martin and placed it on the ground. Then he turned the remote on and started controlling the car. It still worked!

"You fixed it!" Martin exclaimed.

"Yeah, I've dropped my remote a few times already. Dad showed me how to fix it. Emma has also dropped my remote a few times. It's no big deal," Nelson said.

Emma was Nelson's little sister. Just like Nathaniel and Dennis, she loved playing with her big brother's toys. Suddenly, Martin felt bad about how he talked to his brothers.

"What did you do when Emma dropped the remote?" Martin asked.

"At first, I got mad. I yelled at her and it made her cry. Then Dad showed me how easy it was to fix the remote. After that, Dad told me that I should apologize to Emma for yelling at her," Nelson said.

"Why did you have to apologize?"

"Dad said that I should learn how to be empathic. That means that you can try to understand the feelings of others. He asked me how I thought Emma must have felt after I yelled at her. She already felt bad for breaking my remote. When I yelled at her, it made her feel worse."

Martin realized that the same thing happened to his brothers. Even though they apologized to him, he still yelled at them. He even called them the worst brothers in the world. Now that he thought about it, Martin felt bad.

"Is something wrong?" Nelson asked.

"Yes. I need to go home for a while. I just yelled at my brothers for breaking my remote. Now that I think about it, they must be feeling very sad. I should go home and talk to them," he said.

"That's a good idea. Then you should bring them over so we can all play together."

"I will," Martin promised.

Then the little boy went home to talk to his little brothers. After learning what empathy meant, he realized that it was important to think about other people's feelings too.

Showing Respect

Kindness and respect go a long way. The way you treat others is how you end up being treated.
—HEATHER BENNETT-SMALLWOOD

Sam is a young boy who loves to draw. He started drawing when he was just three years old and has gotten very good at it. The little boy has even joined drawing competitions where he won many awards.

Sam was very confident with his drawing abilities. His parents were very proud of him too. But when other people said something bad about his drawings, the little boy got very upset.

"Sam, I heard from one of the parents at your school that there will be a special art class for children next week," Mom said. "Maybe you would like to join."

"But I'm already good at drawing," said the little boy.

"I know you are. But this is a special art class where you can learn some cool new drawing techniques."

Sam thought about it for a while. He loved drawing and learning new things that could make him better sounded fun. So the little boy agreed to join the class.

"That's great! I'll sign you up right away. The class starts in two days," Mom said.

To prepare for the class, the little boy practiced drawing. He wanted to show the teacher that he was the best one in class. Sam was very proud of his drawing skills. For the next two days, he kept drawing to become even better.

On the first day of the special art class, Sam felt excited. Mom dropped him off at the school and wished him luck. He thanked his mom and searched for the room where the special art class was going to happen.

When he found the room, Sam went inside. There were tables with cool art supplies on them. A few children were already sitting in the room. The little boy found an empty seat in front to sit on.

Moments later, a tall man came into the classroom. He was wearing a black shirt, black pants, and shiny black shoes. The man had a long mustache and his hair was short, curly, and messy.

"Good morning, everyone," he said. "My name is Alyster and I will be your teacher for this class."

Sam joined the rest of the class as they greeted Alyster. The little boy felt nervous and excited.

He wondered what kind of techniques he would learn from the teacher.

"Before I start teaching you, I would like to see how good you are at drawing. I want you to take a sheet of paper and draw whatever you want. I will give you some time to do this, then I will go around the class to see what you have made."

Sam felt happy because he wanted to show off his drawing skills. He took a sheet of paper and a pencil, then started drawing. The little boy drew some dinosaurs with a prehistoric background to match.

When he was done, he beamed with pride. Sam looked around and saw that all the other students were still busy drawing. He looked at Alyster and saw that he was busy reading something.

Since he was already finished, Sam looked at the different art materials that were on the table in front of him. There were different types of pencils, crayons, and different types of paint too. Everything was so cool!

Moments later, Alyster stood up, and said, "Time's up!"

Everyone put their pencils down. Alyster walked around the room and checked each of their drawings. When he arrived at Sam's table, he picked up the little boy's paper. Alyster looked at Sam's drawing for a while, then smiled.

He said, "This is good. But you can become even better with all of the new techniques I will show you."

Right away, Sam's smile disappeared. He didn't expect the teacher to say that his drawing was just good.

"My drawing is amazing. You're wrong," he said grumpily.

"Excuse me?" Alyster asked.

"You're wrong. I don't think you're really an art teacher. I am very good at drawing," he said.

Then the little boy stomped out of the room. He went outside, sat on the steps going up to the school, and waited for his mom to pick him up. Since the class had just started, Sam waited a long time for Mom to come.

When she finally arrived at the school, she saw the little boy sitting on the steps.

"Hi! Did the class finish early?" she asked.

"No, I left early," Sam said.

"Why? What happened?" Mom asked.

Still feeling angry, Sam told her what happened. He told her about his drawing and how proud he felt afterward. Then the little boy told her what his teacher said and what he said to his teacher.

"You talked back to your teacher?" asked Mom.

"Yes. He was wrong about my drawing. I'm great at drawing, but he said I was just good."

Mom sat down next to the little boy. She put her arm around him and said, "I understand that you are upset and I understand why. But talking back to your teacher who is much older than you wasn't the right thing to do."

"But... he was wrong!" Sam exclaimed.

"Even if you think he was wrong, you should have respected his opinion," Mom said.

"What do you mean? What is respect?"

"Respect is something that we all need to have towards other people. You show respect by using good words and talking to other people politely. If you feel upset or angry, you should still speak politely, especially when you're talking to people who are older than you," Mom explained.

"But I didn't like what he said about my drawing," Sam said.

"I understand that. But when he talked to you about your drawing, did he say it in a bad way?" Mom asked.

"Well... no. He was smiling when he said that my drawing was good. Then he said that I can be even better after learning some techniques from him," Sam remembered.

"I see. That's a great example of showing respect. Even though your teacher is much older than you, he still spoke to you respectfully," Mom said.

Sam thought about what Mom said for a while. He also thought about what happened in the class. Alyster didn't say anything bad about Sam's drawing. He even said that it was good. But Sam wanted to impress his teacher so much. He wanted the teacher to say that his drawing was the best in the class.

Before he knew it, he got upset. Then he talked back at his teacher. Nobody else did that. All the other children in the class listened to what Alyster had to say.

"Do you remember how excited you were about learning new things? That's why you agreed to join the class, right?" Mom reminded the little boy.

Sam nodded.

"Alyster is an art teacher. His saying that your drawing was good means that he was impressed.

But he also wants you to learn more so that you can be better," Mom explained.

Sam nodded again. He knew that Mom was right. He also realized that talking back to his teacher and not showing him respect was wrong.

"I think I should go inside and apologize," he said.

"That's a good idea," Mom agreed.

Sam stood up and so did his mom. But when he turned around, he saw that all the other children from the art class were walking out of the school. The class was finished and they were all talking excitedly about the first lesson they had.

The little boy took a step forward, then stopped. Alyster was walking towards them. When he saw Sam, the teacher smiled.

"Here you are. I was worried about you when you didn't come back to the classroom," he said.

Sam didn't know how to answer. He looked at mom and she smiled at him warmly. The little boy took a deep breath and looked up at his teacher.

"I'm sorry for what I said. I was upset, but I should have been respectful. I just wanted to impress you so much. But when you said that my drawing was just good and not the best one in the class, it made me mad. Still, I shouldn't have talked back," Sam said.

Alyster smiled at the little boy, "Thank you for apologizing. Just so you know, I don't usually call drawings good unless they really are amazing. Through your drawing, I saw how talented you are. That's why I was excited to teach you new things."

The teacher's words made Sam feel better. He promised to go back to class the next day and be respectful all the time. Since then, Sam learned a lot and became one of the best students in the class.

IT'S TIME TO APPLY WHAT YOU HAVE LEARNED!

Did you have fun reading the stories?

Which was your favorite tale?

Who was your favorite character?

By now, you would have already learned many new values that will help you become a good little boy. Each of these stories had a lesson to share and hopefully, you understood what those lessons meant.

Now, it's time to practice what you have learned. Show your dad, mom, teachers, and everyone else around you how kind, confident, and responsible you are. As you do this, you will feel happier because you will make other people happy too.

And if you happen to forget something, all you have to do is to read these stories again to help you remember!

THANK YOU

A thousand times thank you for purchasing my book!

There is always a risk in purchasing a book that might not suit you.

I could not be anymore grateful you had an opportunity to read all the stories in my book.

As a small favor I would like to ask you if you could please consider leaving a review on the platform? This would really humble independent authors like me a lot.

Any good feedback is very much appreciated and will help in the process of making more great short stories. Again, Thanks!

>> Review Link Amazon US <<

>> Review Link Amazon UK <<

REFERENCES

Be strong quotes. (n.d.). Brainy Quote. https://www.brainyquote.com/topics/be-strong-quotes

Cullins, A. (n.d.). *41 Confidence quotes to inspire children.* Big Life Journal. https://biglifejournal.com/blogs/blog/confidence-quotes

50 Powerful education quotes for kids to realize the importance of learning. (2022, January 17). Splash Learn. https://www.splashlearn.com/blog/powerful-education-quotes-for-kids-to-realize-the-importance-of-learning/

40 Self honesty quotes for kids, relationships & more. (2021, December 5). Turtle Quotes. https://turtlequote.com/self-honesty-quotes-for-relationship/

Hofstaedter, M. (2015, May 15). *Great responsibility quotes hor kids.* Inspire My Kids. https://inspiremykids.com/great-responsibility-quotes-for-kids/

Inner strength for children quotes (4 Quotes). (n.d.). Goodreads. https://www.goodreads.com/quotes/tag/inner-strength-for-children

Joshi, S. (2021, June 16). *115 Great respect quotes for kids.* Mom Junction. https://www.momjunction.com/articles/teach-respect-quotes-for-kids_00747387/

McKay, R. (n.d.). *15 Best quotes about dreaming big.* New Idea. https://www.newidea.com.au/dream-quotes

Price-Mitchell, M. (2019, February 25). *Kindness quotes that teach kids to care.* Roots of Action. https://www.rootsofaction.com/kindness-quotes-kids/

Sarah. (2021, July 22). *51 Inspirational quotes for kids to skyrocket self esteem.* One Mum & a Little Lady. https://onemumandalittlelady.com/inspirational-quotes-for-kids/

Stutman, M. (2016, November 11). *Great empathy quotes for kids and students.* Inspire My Kids. https://inspiremykids.com/great-empathy-quotes-kids-students-children/

Tigers, L. (2022, December 10). *100 Best confidence quotes for kids to inspire.* https://liltigers.net/confidence-quotes-for-kids/

Made in the USA
Middletown, DE
30 September 2024

61693329R20076